Vampire Girl

Lenny Lee

INTRODUCTION

Natalie Silks is a young twelve-year-old girl who loves
going to school, spending time with her friends, and
having quality time with her parents. But lately, Natalie
has been spending less and less time doing the things she
once loved but instead is spending more time in her
room. That's because Natalie has a secret! Natalie has
invited a vampire to live in her home without anyone
knowing.

Vampires have been banished from Natalie's city for
hundreds of years, but when Natalie met the distressed
Amethyst one day in the park, she knew that she would
do anything in her power to protect the young vampire
girl. When people started going missing around Natalie's
city and Amethyst is the alleged culprit, Natalie and
Amethyst go to great lengths to clear the vampire's
name.

"Vampire Girl" is a story of determination, strength, and
why people should not judge a book by its cover.

CHAPTER ONE

It was a sunny afternoon as Natalie Silks raced home from school. The twelve-year-old didn't even stop when Mrs. Robinson greeted her from across the street. The red-haired girl with freckles merely waved her hand.

"Hi Mrs. Robinson!" the young girl called out from across the street, not breaking her stride. It was her mission to make it home. Most little girls and boys hurried home on a school day just to be done with school, but not Natalie. All of her friends were at school, and she loved to learn. No, there was something even more special waiting at home for her. Something that even her parents did not know about.

"Well, be careful!" Mrs. Robinson screamed. The young girl was definitely in a hurry, and the woman could see that Natalie was too busy to play with Cory, Mrs. Robinson's adorable Shiatsu.

"I have to make it home and quickly!" Natalie said as she paused to catch her breath. Running home from school wasn't an easy feat, but she didn't want to keep her friend waiting. Natalie thought back on that fateful day two weeks ago.

Natalie was riding her bike through the park not too far from her house after begging her mom and dad to let her ride her bike. Their town was the safest town in the entire world, and everyone knew everyone, so her parents did not have to worry about Natalie getting mixed into the wrong crowd or coming across bad people.

Natalie enjoyed riding her bike in the park. She could ride her bike as fast as she could without worrying about crashing into anyone because most people worked during the day. She loved how the wind danced in her hair and how the cool breeze softly caressed her cheeks. Natalie was having a blast but came to an immediate stop when she heard sniffling.

"He... hello?" Natalie called out hesitantly. She wasn't expecting anyone to be in the park because nobody ever was at that time of day. She wasn't planning to come across someone crying.

"Leave me alone," a soft voice sounded all around Natalie. Natalie looked around when she realized that the sound appeared to belong to a girl.

"I won't hurt you," Natalie said as she saw a slight movement coming from behind a nearby bush. Whoever the girl was, she sounded sad, and Natalie wouldn't forgive herself if she just left someone who was apparently in distress.

"Humans are all the same," the voice said, and a loud sniffle followed behind the cruel words that shook Natalie's heart. "All you care about is fighting off beings unlike you!" the young girl shouted.

Are all humans the same? Natalie immediately thought. If the girl thought that humans were the same, it was apparent that the girl who was crying was not a human. Mystical beings weren't a fairy tale anymore. Humans had come to terms with the existence of supernatural beings some hundred years ago. Humans still feared them slightly, but they had welcomed them with slightly trembling opened arms.

Natalie got close enough to the peek into the darkened bush. She could barely see, but what she could make out was a ghostly pale girl with long, dark hair with her face in her hands.

"All humans are not the same," Natalie said cautiously, pushing some of the shrubberies away so that she could see the girl better. "There can only be one Natalie Silks! And Natalie Silks is one of the nicest and friendliest people I know!" Natalie said, reassuring the sad girl. The girl wiped at her eyes and moved her eyes to meet Natalie's brown ones. Natalie gasped in shock. The girl's irises were crimson red! A vampire?! Natalie thought to herself in shock. Mostly all supernatural beings were accepted by humans: werewolves, ghosts, trolls, and wizards, but the most feared of them all were vampires! Creatures that preyed on humans!

"Well, Natalie Silks," the young pale-faced vampire said. "If all humans are not the same, why do you cower in fear at the sight of me? I haven't done anything to you. If anything, you've disturbed me!"

Natalie was slightly taken aback when she found out that the young girl was a vampire. There were so many horrible rumors about vampires that it would take her days to list all of the stories! But Natalie couldn't just walk away from someone in need.

"I was afraid, but I'm more afraid to think that you're out here by yourself crying without someone to comfort you," Natalie said sincerely, and the vampire girl arched her brow in confusion.

"Human…no…. Natalie Silks, I was not expecting to hear you say such kind words. Is a human taking pity on a vampire? That is a first for my kind."

"That's because there are those who are not as understanding as me," Natalie responded. "Please tell me what's wrong. I'll listen to you all you want!" the red-haired human girl said enthusiastically. The vampire girl closed her eyes in deep thought. After a while, she emerged from inside of the bushes and looked Natalie in her eyes with her sad crimson ones.

"My name is Amethyst, and I'm a vampire." It was on

that day that Amethyst had shared her story with Natalie and Natalie knew right then and there that she would always be there for the vampire.

Natalie shook her head as she stopped reminiscing. Her house was in sight, and she knew that her parents were not home yet. Natalie unlocked her front door with a grin spreading across her face as she entered the house.

"Amethyst, I'm home!"

***

"So, humans are in school all day just listening to someone talk?" Amethyst's eyes widened in wonder as Natalie told her what happened at school that day.

"Well… not all day. We read to ourselves and work on group projects. Plus, there's recess," Natalie said, as she listed other things that happened at her school.

"Humans have such complex lives," Amethyst said as she shook her head allowing her dark hair to flow in the air.

"What are schools like for vampires?" Natalie asked. Amethyst rarely spoke about herself; the vampire girl was more interested in Natalie's life.

"Well… there aren't any schools for vampires," Amethyst responded after a few moments. "We are either self-taught because of our high IQs, homeschooled by another vampire, or we disguise ourselves as humans and go to humans' schools." Amethyst shook her head. "However, disguising ourselves as humans does not work anymore as far as schools are concerned."

"Yeah," Natalie said sadly. When vampires were run out of the city because humans feared them and refused to cohabit with them, concoctions and new technology were developed to ensure that vampires did not live amongst them. Amethyst managed to avoid detection because of Natalie's help; however, Amethyst spent most of her days alone and hidden in Natalie's bedroom.

"Don't feel bad," Amethyst said, noting Natalie's saddening mood. Natalie was not at fault with Amethyst's and her people's situation. The responsibility lay in the misunderstanding between humans and vampires. Vampires were never honestly given a chance to live in a world peacefully with humans, so it was only inevitable that things had turned out this way.

"Still…" Natalie said pouting. "Everyone should have the right to an education. I mean… werewolves attend my school! How can humans fear vampires and not werewolves?" Natalie shook her head. As far as the dangerous scale goes, to Natalie, vampires, and werewolves were equally as dangerous. She didn't want humans to discriminate against werewolves, she just thought about how hypocritical and unfair the whole situation was.

"Yes, but luckily for me I have access to all your books and your Internet when everyone is gone," Amethyst said and grinned. Amethyst's crimson eyes sparkled, and Natalie couldn't help but grin as well. "I can learn what you're learning and much more on my own time. The best part of everything is that I'm not forced to do it!" Natalie was happy that Amethyst said that, the human girl would have remained sad if she thought her friend was in pain.

"Well, if I look at things from your perspective, I guess I'm pretty jealous!" Natalie beamed. "I love school, but I have my days that I'd prefer to be somewhere other than school." Natalie could see the benefits of being a vampire; however, the cons outweighed the pros.

"So… continue. What happened with Jenna and Megan?" Amethyst asked, and Natalie continued her story enthusiastically.

CHAPTER TWO

After dinner, Natalie and her parents sat down on the couch and watched TV together. She wanted to go back to her bedroom and try to speak to Amethyst before her parents came upstairs, but she and her parents had this thing where they spend some quality time together after dinner. Natalie used to love this quality time, but now since she was hiding Amethyst in her room, she didn't want to be away from the girl for too long.

"Work is getting to be longer and longer these days," Brandon Silks, Natalie's father, said as he stood up and stretched out his long arms. "I'm thinking about taking a vacation to clear my mind." Natalie wasn't paying too much attention to her parents' conversation, but her ears perked up at that.

"Darling, I've been telling you to take a vacation for the last several weeks," Kristin Silks, Natalie's mother, said rubbing her husband's arm. "You're always so tired when you get home, and you've barely got enough sleep with the amount of work you bring home," Kristin continued. Even Natalie's young mind knew that her father was overworking himself, but him being home on vacation would be problematic for Natalie and Amethyst.

"Mom, dad... aren't you two overreacting?" Natalie said quickly. "Dad looks like he could conquer the whole world in a day and still have enough energy to finish his work!" Both Brandon and Kristin looked at their daughter with confusion apparent on their faces.

"Natalie.... I think you've been looking at the wrong person," Brandon said, shaking his head.

"Yeah sweetie, you even mentioned a few weeks ago that you wished your father would rest more," Kristin said, and Natalie bit her lip. That was before Amethyst moved in! The young girl thought to herself. She needed to do something to keep her father from taking a vacation.... well, from at least taking a vacation where he was at home most of the time.

"Well... yeah," Natalie said as her mind tried to think of something to say to better the situation in her favor. "I guess dad does look a bit tired, but I think maybe dad should go on one of his fishing trips! He's always relaxed after a fishing trip! Why stay at home during a vacation? Why not relax by doing something you love?" Natalie responded. She knew that her father often took fishing trips when he was burned out from work. This'll be a good time to do that! Besides, Natalie's father always brought home the best fish from his trips!

"Well…. I enjoy sleeping as well. I haven't been getting much of that recently." Natalie bit her lip again. Shoot! That didn't work! "But…. a fishing trip does sound good though. Camping out for a few days doesn't seem that bad. I'll be able to get plenty of rest." Natalie's mom frowned at that.

"Darling, I know you like to go fishing, but I think that this time you should just stay home and rest." Natalie looked at her mother in sheer horror. Just when she had come up with the perfect plan to keep her father away from home, her mom stepped in to negate her hard work!

"Mom… you know dad does not do well completely cooped up in the house. He always has to do something 'productive.' A vacation shouldn't be used sleeping all day at home! It should be used to relax while doing something you love!" Natalie countered. She knew that she was acting suspicious, but if her father were home all day, Amethyst wouldn't be able to walk around freely.

Kristin looked at her daughter and frowned. "I thought you loved it when your father is home? You were saying last month that you wanted to spend more time with him when you're home from school." Kristin couldn't understand the change in Natalie. Natalie sure has been acting strange the past few weeks. I wonder what's going on with her. Kristin thought to herself.

"Yeah, sweetheart," Brandon decided to add his two cents. "You used to love it when I surprised you by being home when you come home from school. Are you at that age now?" Brandon didn't elaborate on the meaning behind his latter question, but Natalie knew the unspoken truth. Natalie wasn't getting anywhere with her attempts, so she decided to play it smarter with her next words.

"No dad, that's not it. I just wanted you to do something special with your time off. I didn't mean to make you feel bad," Natalie said feeling defeated; however, she was still very much sincere. Natalie stood up then; she'd regroup later with a more thought out plan. "I'm tired, so I'm going to head to bed." Natalie knew that her parents would be downstairs for at least another two hours. She wanted to use this time with Amethyst.

"Goodnight sweetheart," Kristin stood and gave Natalie a hug and a kiss goodnight.

"Night mom," Natalie wrapped her arms snuggly around her mother.

"See you in the morning," Brandon said, and Natalie quickly bent down to plant a quick kiss on her father's forehead.

"I love you!" Natalie said and scurried to her bedroom. When she arrived, she was happy to see that Amethyst was waiting for her. The best friends talked about anything they could think of before Natalie got into bed and Amethyst vanished out of sight at the sound of Natalie's parents coming up the stairs to turn in for the night.

"Good night, Amethyst," Natalie whispered into the darkness. She didn't know where Amethyst had disappeared to, she could no longer feel her presence, but she knew the vampire girl was nearby.

"Goodnight, Natalie," A low voice resonated throughout the room. Natalie smiled and closed her eyes, happy that Amethyst was safe in her home for another day.

***

"So, these recent disappearances have gotten the small city on edge, Diane."

Natalie walked downstairs as she stretched out yawning over the news anchor's voice. Natalie didn't like the news because the bad news always outweighed the good news.

"I know Tom, and so close to home," the newswoman, Diane, said. "People are disappearing without a trace. No evidence, footprints, or signs of a struggle have been left at the scene of the crime," Diane continued. "We've even had one person disappear here in the same manner!" Natalie stopped and listened as the news reported disappearances in the city. It was odd to Natalie that a crime had taken place in her town because of how safe the city was. Anybody in the city could have their doors unlocked at home, leave for a week, and come back to their house in the same manner they left it.

"There have been rumors going around at the office of the disappearances," Brandon said as he and Kristin watched the news together. "Everyone seems to believe that a supernatural being is behind these disappearances! The victim from our city is Kevin Walsh." Kevin Walsh? Natalie thought to herself. She didn't know the man herself, but she knew that Mr. Walsh was Amy's father. That explains why Amy hasn't been to school recently!

"Amelia says it has to be the work of the vampires! Nobody, human or not, can pull off a kidnapping like this with no evidence. It is expected that the vampires have come together to get revenge on the city for banishing them!" Kristin said, shaking her head. She didn't believe the rumors at first, but since more people were disappearing, she was starting to feel there was some truth to it.

Natalie couldn't believe what she was hearing. How could people automatically assume the disappearances was the work of vampires? Natalie could understand why people would think vampires wanted revenge, but after spending so much time with Amethyst and getting to know her, she learned that vampires are not as scary or evil as everyone believes. They were kind beings.

"They're wrong!" Natalie said without thinking. Her parents turned towards her and looked at her in confusion. "I'm sure that vampires are not the ones behind this! Everyone is saying this just because they want to play the blame game!"

"And how would you know young lady?" Brandon asked. "Vampires have been banished from this city since before you and I were born. How would you know what the vampires' agenda is?" Natalie bit her lip. Me and my big mouth! I can't tell them that an actual vampire told me about vampires!

"School and you have always told me to not judge a book by its cover or not to listen to rumors blindly. I truly believe humans were just afraid of vampires to the point they felt the need to make something up about vampires to ease their ignorance." It was rare that Natalie jumped into a grown-up conversation, but in this case, Natalie felt the need to come to Amethyst's and her fellow vampires' defense.

"Darling," Brandon stood up then and walked over to his daughter. He had never seen the young girl so worked up about something. "I'm glad you are taking what you were taught and what you believe into consideration, but this situation," Brandon thought as he shook his head. "Given all of the traits, we do know regarding humans and supernatural beings…only vampires could pull off a disappearing act like this with no traces left behind."

"Natalie," Kristin nodded her head in agreement with her husband. "You're still so young. We understand where you're coming from, and that you have a good heart and soul. But sometimes people with the best intentions could be wrong. There's no solid evidence that a vampire is behind these disappearances, but there is no evidence against it." Natalie felt like her parents were the ones who were not getting the picture, but she decided to bite her tongue and stop talking.

"I forgot something in my room," Natalie didn't want to push the conversation any longer than it needed to be. If she admitted to how she was sure her information was correct, Natalie would surely be punished for lying to her parents. Natalie walked up the stairs to her bedroom and heard her TV playing as she got closer to her room.

Natalie was confused when she approached her door because she was sure that she hadn't left her TV on because she and Amethyst hadn't watched TV that morning. Opening the door, she was surprised to see Amethyst's back towards her with a brilliant sketch of a picture of Amethyst on the TV screen.

CHAPTER THREE

"Amethyst... what's... what's this?" Natalie lowered her voice and quickly closed and locked her door. Why is a picture of Amethyst on the screen?! Natalie thought to herself.

"I heard you and your parents talking about the disappearing humans and how everyone thought that vampires were behind it. When I turned on the news station... this is what I saw," Amethyst said waving her hand towards the TV.

"But... why would they have a picture of you? Why are you linked to the disappearances?" Natalie had a lot of questions for Amethyst. She couldn't understand how someone could have seen her when she's never left Natalie's house since she "moved" the vampire girl in.

"Please don't be mad," Amethyst said quietly as she turned to look at Natalie. Whatever Amethyst was going to say, Natalie was sure that she was not going to like it. "Sometimes, I'm so bored at night that I sneak out when everyone's sleeping."

"You what?" Natalie yelled, barely able to hold back her voice. Amethyst shushed Natalie and walked closer to the infuriated girl.

"I am so bored and lonely when you go to sleep, so I leave for maybe thirty minutes and go to the park. It's always around 2 or 3 in the morning, and I never see anybody out and about during that time in the park," Amethyst said placing her hands on Natalie's shoulders. The vampire could tell that Natalie was angry.

"Well apparently someone was out because they saw you!" Natalie couldn't believe that Amethyst did this. Amethyst knew that if she were caught in town, she would be punished severely. How could the young vampire do this when Natalie was working hard to make sure the girl was safe?

"I know, and I can't even imagine when someone could have possibly seen me," Amethyst said turning back to the TV. "The news anchor said someone had witnessed me the night the human from this town went missing," Amethyst said with a sad voice and Natalie couldn't help but gasp.

"Do they think you're behind it?" Natalie asked in shock; however, she already knew the answer to her question before Amethyst confirmed it.

"Yes, it appears I am the only sighting of a vampire in

town for decades," Amethyst shook her head, and her long flowing jet-black hair swung loosely behind her head. "I'm so sorry. If I hadn't been so careless, this wouldn't have happened." Natalie could instantly feel her anger subsiding. The freckled-face girl had been insensitive before. Of course, Amethyst would be bored locked up in Natalie's house all day. If Natalie were in Amethyst's shoes, she would probably need a change of scenery now and then as well.

"No, don't be sorry," Natalie said after a while. "I'm sorry that I got angry with you, I wasn't thinking. You've done nothing wrong," Natalie said, walking over to Amethyst. The young human girl looked at the vampire in her deep red eyes before embracing her slightly trembling body. It wasn't long before Amethyst returned the embrace.

"I didn't do it," Amethyst whispered, and Natalie nodded her head.

"I know, and I'll make sure everyone else knows as well." Amethyst moved away from Natalie and looked at the girl in confusion.

"How are you going to do that? I know you are keeping me in hiding, but if I go out now, I'll be captured." Amethyst believed that she was a strong vampire and could quickly shake off a few humans. However, she was still a young girl at the end of the day.

"I don't know yet, but surely we'll think of something."

Natalie was an optimistic girl. Even if Amethyst hadn't told Natalie that she hadn't done anything wrong, Natalie would have automatically guessed that the young vampire was innocent. It was terrible that humans were willing to assume that vampires were the culprit, and Natalie wanted to vouch for them without bringing to their attention that she was harboring a vampire in her room. Now that someone had seen Amethyst and the charge was thrown in her direction, Natalie couldn't just sit back and do nothing.

"You are different from the others," Amethyst noted. Amethyst couldn't understand why Natalie was going out of her way to keep her safe. She never knew that she could encounter a human that was sympathetic to her and other vampires. If the vampires had someone like Natalie those many years ago, maybe vampires and humans would have been able to live together in peace.

"Anything for my best friend," Natalie said, exposing small white teeth. They were going to think of a way to clear Amethyst's name. Both were smart girls. The hardest part would be finding evidence to prove Amethyst's innocence without being spotted by anyone.

Natalie didn't know where to begin, but she did know that she'd do anything in her power to make sure that the kind-hearted Amethyst was safe.

***

"You sure we should be doing this?" Amethyst asked as

she and Natalie walked through the abandoned park late at night. Natalie had to admit that she was afraid to be outside this late, especially with the kidnappings going on. Natalie didn't expect that vampires were the culprits, but she did assume that this could potentially be a dangerous trip. Plus, Natalie could get in serious trouble with her parents. She wasn't the type of girl to go against her parents' rules, but in this case, she felt she was justified.

"No, I'm not sure we should be doing this," Natalie answered honestly. "But it'll be a matter of time before you are found. I want to clear your name before then to avoid any additional misunderstandings," Natalie said with confidence. Natalie and Amethyst were in the park looking for clues. Since the park was where Amethyst was spotted at, and allegedly where Mr. Walsh's disappearance had occurred, the girls felt this was the best investigation site.

"I think we should go back," Amethyst said dejectedly. "I appreciate everything that you've done for me thus far, Natalie. You showed me humans could be amazing and understanding to other beings, but…" Amethyst trailed off as she collected her thoughts. Natalie stopped walking then and looked at her best friend. "Go back home. You shouldn't risk your safety for me anymore. I'll walk you back home, and I'll leave this place for good."

"No!" Natalie said quickly and firmly. "I will fight for you no matter what. I won't stand by and allow the people of this town to search for you like you're some deranged animal." Natalie was shouting, but at that moment she didn't care. "Please don't give up, Amethyst. We can prove your innocence together. We can show them that not all vampires are evil."

Amethyst sighed. Amethyst didn't want Natalie getting into trouble on her behalf. How can two young girls, one vampire, and one human, prove to the world that vampires are not monsters? Amethyst wanted to refuse the girl's help, but she was happy with Natalie's loyalty.

"Alright, Natalie. I'm thankful to have someone like you in my life. Even though I think your efforts will be in vain, I will help you try to clear my name." Natalie grinned at that. She didn't like that Amethyst was so pessimistic about the whole thing, but Natalie believed that Amethyst's attitude would change once they had enough evidence that proved Amethyst's, and all vampires', innocence.

"We can do this!" Natalie shouted enthusiastically, and Amethyst shushed her. "Okay, can you sense anyone here?" Natalie asked, and Amethyst closed her eyes in concentration. She was able to sense other beings; however, since she was still young, it took a lot of effort. After a few moments, Amethyst shook her head.

"No, there is nobody here," Amethyst closed her eyes again. "I sense that people have been at the park for the last few days, and I also sense myself. I do not sense that any vampires have been here at all though," Amethyst said, turning to Natalie.

"Can you tell when's the last time a vampire other than yourself has been here?" Natalie asked. This was good to know. Mr. Walsh went missing the other day, and hearing Amethyst say that vampires hadn't been here in the past few days was comforting.

"I'm not that powerful yet when it comes to sensing others, but I can tell you that vampires, other than myself, have not been here in the past few months."

"There you have it!" Natalie said feeling proud, but Amethyst shook her head.

"You and I know the truth, but you know that the others would only think that makes me more likely the suspect since I was the only vampire in the park during the time the human went missing," Amethyst said, opening her eyes. "I have nothing to do with that man's disappearance, but that proves nothing."

"You're right," Natalie said. "To everyone else, you're still the likely suspect; however, you've proved to you and me that a vampire was not behind it!" Natalie said confidently. Natalie didn't expect to get that many clues right away that would prove Amethyst's innocence, but the fact that Amethyst confirmed that other than her, vampires had not been near the park, shows that the town placed the blame on vampires prematurely.

"Yes, but we need to find concrete information to prove

to the humans," Amethyst said with a sigh, and Natalie nodded her head.

"Let's look for as much information as we can," Natalie said as she started to look around the park. She was sure that they were going to find the information that they needed. No matter what everyone else is saying about vampires, Natalie believed in her vampire best friend. No matter how unreasonable the town people get, Natalie and Amethyst would end up proving to them that they're wrong. They needed to try their best and work together.

Amethyst looked over at the overconfident girl and couldn't help but grin. "Thank you, Natalie."

CHAPTER FOUR

Natalie was extremely tired when she woke up to the sound of her mother's voice and knocking on her door.

"Natalie… Natalie! Why is your door locked?" Natalie was wide awake then.

"Oh, sorry!" Natalie said as she jumped up out of her bed and rushed to her bedroom door. Natalie opened the door to her mother looking down at her with her hands on her hips.

"Why do you have your door locked? What are you hiding in here?" Kristin asked curiously as she looked around her daughter's room. Natalie had been acting strange lately and had her bedroom door locked only cast more suspicion on the young girl.

"I didn't mean to lock my door, I must have done it without thinking," Natalie said quickly. She knew her excuse didn't sound too convincing; she didn't even convince herself.

"Your behavior recently has been quite peculiar. What's going on with you?" Kristin asked. She had spoken with her husband about Natalie's recent behavior, and he said it was probably due to her growing up. When Brandon and Kristin were growing up, they started telling their parents less and less and were not as open with them any longer. Brandon assumed that this was beginning to be the case with Natalie, but Kristen didn't buy his explanation. Something was going on with Natalie, and Kristin was going to find out.

"Nothing mom," Natalie said a little hesitantly. When her mother had a certain opinion on something, getting her to change her mind was like asking a tree to grow legs and walk. Impossible! "Honestly, I don't even remember locking my door because I have no reason to."

"That's not all I'm talking about, Natalie. For the past couple of weeks, you're spending more and more time in your room, instead of going outside with your friends. You don't spend as much quality time with your father and me after dinner. Something's up, and I want you to know that you can confide in me, darling." Natalie bit her lip.

"I didn't realize I was acting so different." Once her mother's words were out there in the open, Natalie could agree that her attempts to keep Amethyst a secret were making the young girl look even more suspicious. Her mother was right about everything that she had said, but Natalie honestly hadn't realized how different she was acting.

"I'm sorry, but nothing's wrong, I didn't even realize I was acting odd." Natalie wanted to tell her mother about Amethyst but now wasn't the time. She knew that she would eventually get in trouble, but Natalie knew that she was going to have to come clean if she was to clear Amethyst's name.

"*Sigh* I'm just letting you know breakfast is ready. I've been calling you for a while, so I came upstairs when you never answered," Kristin said as she looked around Natalie's room again. She didn't like that her daughter was so distant from her, but she wasn't going to pressure Natalie to tell her what's on her mind. Kristin was hoping that in time Natalie would open up to them when she was ready.
"I'll brush my teeth and be down in a few minutes!" Kristen nodded her head and made her way back downstairs. Natalie sighed when she was sure her mother was no longer around and shut her bedroom door.

"Seems like you've been worrying your parents a lot," Amethyst noted as soon as Natalie turned around. Natalie almost gasped in shock. Natalie knew that Amethyst could disappear and reappear at the drop of a hat, but she wasn't expecting the vampire to be behind her. After living with the crimson-eyed girl for a few weeks, Natalie should have been used to Amethyst's vampire abilities.

"I didn't realize that my personality had changed that much," Natalie said honestly. Sure, Natalie knew that she was trying desperately to make sure her father wouldn't stay home during his vacation, and she knew that she hadn't been going out that much, but other than that Natalie didn't think she had looked too suspicious. But now Natalie realized that she had been mistaken.

"Regardless of my situation," Amethyst continued. "You must try to act as natural as possible to avoid further suspicion from your parents." Amethyst could tell that Natalie was starting to feel bad, so the pale-skinned dark-haired beauty gave Natalie the sweetest of smiles. "We won't be able to clear my name and the reputation of vampires if we're caught before we've done any detective work!" Natalie grinned at Amethyst's enthusiastic behavior.

"Right! We can't let our efforts last night fall apart!" Natalie said ecstatically. She'll make it up to her parents and her school friends when everything was over, but right now she needed to work on saving her best friend. "I'm going to brush my teeth and head downstairs to eat. I'll grab you something when my parents leave." Amethyst nodded her head, and in a blink of an eye, she had disappeared.

Natalie made her way towards the bathroom to freshen up to start her day.

***

"So, the man reported seeing you during the same time Mr. Walsh went missing. One moment he saw Mr. Walsh in the park, shortly he saw you, then suddenly both of you were nowhere to be found," Natalie said as she read the news report that spoke about the disappearance of the latest 'alleged' kidnapped victim.

"I didn't sense the human that reported seeing me, which is probably because I'm not strong enough yet," Amethyst said as she thought back to the night that Mr. Walsh had gone missing and her whereabouts that night. "But if someone were, in fact, jogging in the park, I would have heard that. I was out of sight when I was there, but I had a clear visual on the path." This didn't make any sense to Amethyst nor Natalie. How could two people have been in the park and she didn't sense or see either one of them? She's not as strong as her brethren, but she was decent when it came to sensing living beings.

"Something just doesn't add up," Natalie said as she ran her hand through her red hair. The reports she and Amethyst read made no sense. Amethyst had left her vampire clan to make a better life for herself in the city of her ancestors, but before she went, she had been improving all her vampiric skills. Natalie thought the vampire girl was terrific, and there was no way that the young vampire would have slipped up that much. It was evident to her that something wasn't right with what the witness had reported.

"Where do we go from here?" Amethyst asked. "I

cannot go outside during the day because I'm sure to get detected." Natalie thought about that for a few moments. They were really at a loss and wasn't progressing much. However, Natalie was sure that they'd be able to find out something if they had more information on the victim, Mr. Walsh.

"I can give Amy a call!" Natalie shouted. Amy hadn't been in school lately, probably because of her father's disappearance. But if she could somehow get Amy to talk to her, she could find out more information on Amy's father.

"Amy is the daughter of the missing human, correct?" Amethyst asked, and Natalie nodded her head.

"We're not going to find too much information online, and I doubt that the police will talk to a twelve-year-old girl about a missing person case. If we want more information about Mr. Walsh, our best bet is to ask someone close to him." Amethyst thought that Natalie had a good lead on who to talk to, but Amethyst wasn't too sure about the reliability of a young human.

"Well...I'm not sure if this Amy girl will have anything useful, but there is no harm in trying," Amethyst gave Natalie her support. Natalie smiled and ran to get her phone. Finding Amy's number quickly in her contact list, she made the call.

She was sure that Amy and her family had a lot on their plates now, and Natalie knew that she, out of all people, should not be bothering her. Though Natalie wanted any information that could help Amethyst, she was feeling confident that they would end up finding Mr. Walsh and the rest of the victims.

The phone rung several times, and Natalie was starting to lose her enthusiastic attitude. What happens if no one answered because of the numerous reporters who were more than likely still calling? What happens if the family took it upon themselves to search for Mr. Walsh? What if they had caller ID and deemed Natalie's call not important enough? These negative thoughts ran through every corner of Natalie's brain. The young girl was just about to give up when a familiar voice answered the phone with a sad 'hello.'

"Amy!"

CHAPTER FIVE

"Oh...Natalie, my life has been crazy. I miss my daddy," Amy said as she and Natalie spoke on the phone. Natalie told her how sorry she was for her and her family, and that she was sure that her dad would be found safe soon, then Natalie hit her with questions. If Natalie didn't have a childlike voice and Amy didn't already know the young girl, one could have possibly mistaken her for a private detective.

"Everything will be alright, Amy. Your dad will be home soon, and you two will play together, and this will one day become part of the past." Natalie said things she knew her mother would have told someone to make them feel better if they were in a similar situation. She spoke to Amy for a few more minutes about school work, and how Natalie was willing to help Amy in any way before they disconnected. Natalie looked at Amethyst who sat next to her.

"So... there is an inconsistency between what that witness said and what Amy is saying," Amethyst said as she furrowed her perfectly arched eyebrows.

"Yes, there is," Amy told Natalie that her father was home most of the day and got called to meet with a friend for a little while. There would have been no reason for Amy's father to have been at the park, and that he never went to the park because of his allergies. Amy said that her mother had been in such a shock about the entire ordeal that she hasn't responded to any reports or made any comments regarding the news report that had gone out. When Natalie asked what friend called him, Amy mentioned that she was not sure and that her father's phone was nowhere to be found to check.

It didn't take Amethyst long to make her assessment. "The witness lied," Amethyst said. The witness had remained anonymous, so there was no way to ID the man who gave the report. "But… I don't understand why the witness would have lied."

"Are you sure you didn't speak to anyone else when you came to the city? Do you have any personal enemies that I don't know about?" Amethyst didn't even have to think too long about Natalie's questions.

"You are the only being I've spoken to since coming here. I also haven't made any enemies since being here. I'll also have you know that my family is highly respected amongst vampires. It was seldom that we saw other supernatural beings and we never saw humans where we were located. Other than humans, we have no enemies." There is no reason why anyone would have anything personal against Amethyst, but it appeared that they were trying to make her out to be a monster.

"I believe you, I just wanted to make sure again," Natalie said. The witness identified Amethyst as being the culprit because she and the victim were in the park at the same time and both disappeared around the same time. Amethyst never sensed the presence of either the witness or the victim while at the park the day of his disappearance. Amy reported that her father was meeting with an unidentified friend the night he went missing. This information did not provide absolute proof that could be used for the public to stop suspecting Amethyst, but it did give them evidence that the witness had fabricated that night's events.

"Perhaps the witness and the 'friend' are the same individuals?" Amethyst responded slowly as she tried to find ways the witness and the friend were related. This 'friend' has not reached out to the police yet, even though they were more than likely the last one who contacted the victim. There were so many plot holes in this case.

"Probably, and it'll take too long to try to hunt down all of Mr. Walsh's friends," Natalie said. Though the town was small enough that everyone knew everyone on a first name basis, the two young girls didn't have enough time to figure out who Mr. Walsh considered a good friend. "Any thoughts on what we should do next?"

Natalie and Amethyst sat on the bed quietly. Now since there was a picture of Amethyst circling the small town, the two girls knew that they didn't have long until

Amethyst was found. They needed to crack this case well before then. Natalie hated the fact that she couldn't think of anything else that could help them. Even though Natalie was determined to prove Amethyst's innocence and spread a positive light on vampires, Natalie was still a young girl who didn't know the entirety of how life worked.

"We can probably go back to the park soon to see if we missed any clues." Amethyst didn't know what else they could do with so little to go on. They were also running out of time to investigate everything. She knew that Natalie meant well, but the young vampire was starting to lose faith in their situation. The longer they took to prove that Amethyst had nothing to do with the recent disappearances, the more likely she would be captured by the humans who were more than likely starting their hunt for her.

"Well... it definitely can't be tonight," Natalie said as she bit her lip. A full moon was expected, and Natalie knew that the werewolves came out to hunt for food during full moons. But that wasn't the reason Natalie was trying to avoid investigating that night. Werewolves' senses are heightened during the full moon. If Natalie and Amethyst got too close to a werewolf, they'd surely sniff out Amethyst. If that happened, the beasts would report Amethyst to the town's officials.

"Ah, yes, the mutts are coming out tonight," Amethyst said, remembering the day. They really couldn't afford to miss any nights when it came to investigating the mysterious disappearances, but Amethyst was no fool. The two of them couldn't get away from a werewolf no matter how hard they tried. Not wanting to make Natalie feel sad, Amethyst smiled at her. "Don't worry; everything will work out." Natalie nodded her head.

Natalie didn't know exactly what the two of them could do, and now that time was running out she was becoming more nervous. However, no matter how much the odds were looking against them, they had to do something!

***

It was a few nights later before Natalie and Amethyst were able to investigate the park again. The effects of the full moon lasted longer than usual, so they had to ensure that Amethyst was as far away from werewolves as possible. Natalie looked around cautiously as she navigated through the dark streets trying to see if any pedestrians were walking around who could easily spot her. Amethyst traveled somewhere near Natalie in the shadows. Amethyst didn't make a single sound as the two of them walked through the night.

"You think if there were any more evidence here, that'll it'd be gone now?" Natalie asked quietly. She was nervous and anxious at the same time. The streets had been bustling lately with people going around with Amethyst's pictures on picket signs. It made Natalie sick! Everyone was listening to 'he said, she said' versus going out and finding the truth for themselves.

"I don't know," Amethyst answered from the darkness. "I guess it depends on what kind of evidence was left behind," Amethyst said. Amethyst did not have any first-hand knowledge of the type of evidence humans left behind. If a vampire decided to take the path of a crook, they didn't leave evidence because of how skilled vampires are. So, to an extent, Amethyst understood how the humans quickly assumed vampires might have played a role in the disappearance of the missing humans.

"It doesn't hurt to try at least," Natalie said. It was starting to get a little hard to remain positive, but Natalie knew that she had to try to keep their morale high.

It did not take them long to make it to the park, and Natalie was happy to see that nobody appeared to be there. Natalie strained her eyes through the darkness to make sure that nobody was spying on them.

"We're the only ones here," Natalie said, but then she heard a voice immediately to the right of her, and the red-haired girl almost jumped from shock. Amethyst grinned. "You're not used to that yet?"

"I don't think I could ever get used to you are being able to reappear and disappear soundlessly," Natalie said, placing her hand over her heart in a dramatic matter. Amethyst's fangs sparkled in the moonlight before her facial expression turned serious.

"Let's hurry, I don't want you out here too late," she said. Natalie nodded, and the two of them immediately looked around the park. Natalie looked in the garbage cans, the benches, anywhere she thought she'd be able to find something out of the ordinary, while Amethyst searched high in the trees just in case something of importance was taken there because of the wind.

Amethyst appreciated everything that Natalie had done for her thus far, but the vampire was starting to think that they should possibly call it quits. The more she remained with the human girl, the more likely the girl would be hurt because of her. Maybe... maybe I should leave. Amethyst did not want to bring any pain to her human friend, but obviously, she would not just leave Natalie by herself in the park. After thinking about it briefly, Amethyst decided to leave and never return after Natalie had fallen asleep. Not because Amethyst no longer wished to live amongst humans, but to ensure that Natalie didn't get hurt.

Amethyst immediately was pulled from her thoughts when she heard footsteps from a short distance away. She held her breath and cleared her mind from any other distractions. Amethyst had to make sure she wasn't just paranoid. When Amethyst heard the mumbling of what sounded like a man, she jumped down gracefully from the tree and landed beside Natalie. Before the red-haired girl had a chance to say anything, Amethyst grabbed her and jumped quickly into some bushes nearby.

"Amet...!" Natalie was barely able to get out before a pale hand was pressed firmly to her mouth. Natalie looked up at the vampire confused until she finally heard the sounds that had freaked her best friend out.

"Where has that little vampire girl gone?" Amethyst's crimson and brown eyes went wide when they saw the silhouette of a man standing directly in front of them.

CHAPTER SIX

Natalie squinted her eyes in the darkness to see who the man was, and she was shocked to see it was Mr. Terry. Mr. Terry was known for his... the unconventional way of thinking. He'd never fully accepted living amongst supernatural beings, and he often said, the reason why vampires were no longer living in the city had something to do with his ancestors. But Natalie didn't understand why he was outside in the middle of the park at night.

"I was sure everyone would have grabbed that little leech after the kidnappings. It's the vampire's fault for being here," Mr. Terry kept mumbling, and Natalie found it difficult to understand precisely what the belligerent man was talking about.

"Do you know this human?" Amethyst whispered so low that even though the two girls were close together, Natalie barely heard her.

"Yes, he's sort of like.... a crazy person," Natalie almost forgot to stifle a giggle. The situation they were in was not funny, but she couldn't help but laugh as she saw Mr. Terry flail around like a madman.

"That little vermin has been hiding out in my city, enjoying my park, when her kind is not welcome here. It took all my strength to take all those people without leaving any traces of any wrongdoing to make it look like a vampire has done it!" Natalie and Amethyst couldn't believe their ears as Mr. Terry monologued his plan to bring down Amethyst just because he had happened to see her one day.

Natalie couldn't believe it! They had come here to find some evidence, but they had ended up hitting the jackpot. This was better than good; it was terrific!

"It's a shame that I had to kidnap Kevin too, but he's the only person that speaks to me. I'm sorry I had to do it, but these people were not taking the bait when people were being taken from a different town," Mr. Terry shook his head as he had just thought of something unpleasant, "No, it had to be someone from here, there was no other way."

"Are you hearing this?" Natalie asked, immediately turning from being happy they had figured out who was behind the mysterious disappearances and who was trying to frame Amethyst, into anger at such a horrible reason to do it. "This…man took those people just because he hated the fact that nobody realized you were hiding out here?"

"Yes, it seems like he is really against vampires being here," Amethyst said, nodding her head. Amethyst thought the man was heartless to go to such lengths to get rid of her. She might have been a vampire, a being the man despised, but at the end of the day, vampire or not, she was still a child. Amethyst felt that the man could have been more sensitive towards her being all alone in the park where he first learned of her existence.

Natalie was seething. She couldn't believe the crimes this man had done! He kidnapped several people, and even his friend to get Amethyst captured. This man didn't deserve a gold medal for finding a vampire in a place that had technology that should have detected vampires all over the city. This man deserved jail time for kidnapping, discrimination, and for framing another individual. Natalie couldn't stand a second more of the crazed man's mumbling. She stood up without a second thought, and Amethyst looked up at the determined red-head in sheer horror.

"Natalie! No!" Amethyst was barely able to control the volume of her voice. But it was no use, Natalie was already stomping her way towards the irate human.

"How dare you do something so disgusting just because you don't like something!" The man called Mr. Terry flinched, startled, at the sound of Natalie's screaming voice. Amethyst didn't know what to do; she'd never been so close to a human before other than Natalie. She was afraid to move from her spot, so she remained hidden in the shadows.

41

"Oh my! You gave me quite the spook," Mr. Terry said, relaxing when he noticed that Natalie was a girl he was familiar with, and he knew for a fact that she was human. "It's well past your bedtime, why are you out so late?" Mr. Terry asked, disregarding what the young girl had just said.

"You heard me!" Natalie retorted. She knew what the older man was doing, she had heard everything that he had said, and she wasn't letting him get away with it. "Framing an innocent young girl and kidnapping people just to make lives more difficult for vampires!" Natalie said without holding back. Fresh tears had started to form in her eyes. She was sad to say this, but it seemed to her the evilest creatures to walk this earth as humans!

"Oh, so you know the little leech, do you?" Mr. Terry asked, furrowing his eyebrows. He wasn't planning on his misconduct being found out, but if he had to be found out, he was happy that it was by someone as tiny as Natalie. "You've made friends with the little vampire girl? Is that why I don't see her in these parks no more?" The more questions Mr. Terry asked, the more the man got angrier. A human befriending a vampire? Preposterous!

"I'm the one asking the questions here!" Natalie shouted as she started to shake. She was always told to respect her elders, but she couldn't respect a man like Mr. Terry. Mr. Terry looked around to see if he could spot the young vampire and when he didn't see her, he grinned.

Amethyst might have been young, but Mr. Terry wouldn't underestimate the enemy.

"I wasn't planning on being found out like this kid, so it looks like I'm going to have to do something about you," Mr. Terry said before moving towards Natalie. Natalie gasped when she realized what the man was about to do. She was next in Mr. Terry's grand scheme to shed a bad light on Amethyst!

Before Natalie could scream, Mr. Terry covered the struggling young girl's mouth with his slightly sweating hand, before pulling her under his arm and making a dash for it. The cellphone that Natalie always had on her fell to the ground loudly as the two of them rushed away.

Amethyst shot up quickly in horror as the only human that that did not fear her, or her people were being carried away by a madman. Amethyst was scared at first, but fear no longer remained in her heart. She had to save Natalie!

***

It felt like Amethyst had been running forever as the man sped down the street at top speed in a car she did not recognize, and Amethyst was starting to have problems following them. She was afraid, not because she might get discovered, but because she put her best friend in danger. Amethyst didn't care what happened to her if Natalie was alright. Amethyst clutched Natalie's phone in her hand as she prayed for the safety of her best friend and the other humans that Mr. Terry had taken. It didn't take them long to arrive at an abandoned house in the middle of nowhere.

"You'll never get away with this!" Natalie screamed as Mr. Terry grabbed her wrist and pulled her out of the car. Even though they were far away from town, Mr. Terry couldn't risk being discovered again. Natalie couldn't believe the events that had transpired, but she didn't regret anything. She didn't see Amethyst anywhere, but Natalie was sure that her friend was somewhere close.

"I'm not worried," Mr. Terry said emotionlessly. "Once that vampire child is captured, I'll free all of you, but don't think I plan to stay here," Mr. Terry said as he looked around one last time. Amethyst followed Mr. Terry's movement, but when he went towards the front door, Amethyst quickly circled the back and climbed through a window that happened to be opened.

"Is this where you have everyone?" Natalie asked, trying to get as much information out of Mr. Terry as possible. If she did manage to escape, she had to tell the police as much about the location of the victims and of Mr. Terry as she possibly could. Mr. Terry didn't answer her though; he was tired of her endless chatter. Mr. Terry took Natalie downstairs to a basement, and much to her surprise, there were jail cells all throughout the basement.

"That cell is yours," Mr. Terry said pointing in the

direction of a cell that was open. Natalie's eyes widened when she followed Mr. Terry's pointed finger. Several of the cells were filled with sleeping people! One of which Natalie recognized as being Mr. Walsh!

"You can't do this! You can't do this to these people. You are framing a sweet vampire girl because of your discrimination! Kidnapping people to have people believe this is the work of vampires. Like humans, there are bad vampires. But vampires care about others and are quite humble, kind, and trustworthy!" Amethyst was the only vampire Natalie knew, so she didn't have much to base her opinion on. Natalie was sure though that she was right in her beliefs.

"Hush…. you'll be out in no time. Surely this latest incident will cause more of an uproar. That vampire will be captured, and I'll be a hero. Everyone will be released as soon as that leech is captured." Mr. Terry escorted Natalie towards a cell and closed it quickly before going towards a lone desk in the middle of the room. "I had a witch make me a sleeping concoction that could make a whale sleep in as quickly as thirty seconds," Mr. Terry said as he walked back over towards Natalie. "Be a good girl and drink this."

"No!" Natalie cried out in horror. Where is Amethyst? That was the one thing that kept running through Natalie's head.

"Looks like you left me no choice," Mr. Terry said, and the voice that Natalie had been waiting for finally spoke up.

"No, looks like you left me no choice," the crimson eyed vampire said as Mr. Terry turned around with a diabolical look in his eye when he saw the vampire.

"You..." Mr. Terry growled but was immediately cut off by the sounds of loud footsteps from above. Mr. Terry paused then with a confused expression marring his features. He turned his head to look at Amethyst, and his eyes widened in shock. Standing behind Amethyst were what appeared to be a dozen cops.

"Freeze!"

CHAPTER SEVEN

The police took Natalie, Amethyst, and Mr. Terry to the police department. Mr. Terry was thrown behind bars while the cops questioned Natalie and Amethyst. The people who were kidnapped were driven to the hospital to make sure they were alright, even though Mr. Terry told them that he didn't harm them in any way. Their families were called, and for the most part, the victims were going to have a happy ending.

"I don't think I've ever seen a vampire before," the police chief said, looking over at Amethyst.
"You say that you respect humans, which is why you came to live in this city even though your people were banished? I've never believed everything that was said about vampires. We have werewolves and witches in our city who are outstanding citizens, and they were depicted as eviler than vampires have ever been depicted."

"Will we still be punished for what we did?" Natalie asked. Even though Natalie felt they did nothing wrong, it was still illegal to have housed a vampire. The police chief smiled and shook his head.

"Are you kidding me, you two are heroes! If it weren't for your determination Natalie, and Amethyst's quick thinking to call the police for us to trace your whereabouts, we would have jailed the wrong person!"

"Will I be banished from this place?" Amethyst asked. Amethyst was happy that the police didn't view her any different then what they would have regarded a child of their kind, but Amethyst understood that rules are rules.

"We need to talk to the town officials," the police chief said. "Your courageous and brave actions are more than enough reason to have vampires reevaluated as honest and kind individuals, but that's not solely for us to decide."

"Natalie Patricia Silks!" Natalie flinched at the sound of her name from the familiar voice. Natalie looked towards the entrance of the police station and saw her mother and father walking towards her. Natalie wasn't surprised the police had called her parents and explained to them what had happened, but she knew what she did was still wrong. Hero or not, she had broken many of her parents' rules.

Kristin and Brandon looked briefly over at the crimson eyed vampire girl before taking their daughter into their arms.

"Leaving the house at night sounds like a two-month

punishment for you," Kristin said as she kissed her daughter quickly on the forehead. When Kristin and Brandon got the call at four in the morning about their daughter's nightly excursions, they didn't know what to say. They knew that something was going on with their daughter, but never in their wildest dream would they have suspected this.

"Start talking," Brandon said, looking from Natalie to Amethyst, "both of you." Natalie and Amethyst looked at one another and grinned. No matter what happened, the two young girls were proud of themselves. They had managed to find out the real perpetrator of these heinous crimes and had cleared Amethyst's name. Amethyst was not an evil vampire, she was a hero, and Natalie hoped that in due time humans would trust vampires and allow them to live in the city again.

Natalie wasn't sure what was going to happen to Amethyst now that the whole ordeal was cleared up, but she was confident that Amethyst's bravery would pave the way for vampire equality. Amethyst looked at Natalie and grinned. She was happy that she had someone like Natalie to care about her, and she was pleased that the other girl didn't get hurt. No matter what happened, Amethyst was sure that Natalie would be there for her. And that's why they were best friends.

"Mom... dad," Natalie started. "It all started a few weeks ago when I met Amethyst in the park."

CHARLIE
BOOK

Made in United States
Orlando, FL
07 October 2022

23117159R00039